Published by Ladybird Books Ltd
80 Strand London WC2R ORL
A Penguin Company

4 6 8 10 9 7 5 3

LADYBIRD and the device of a ladybird are trademarks of Ladybird Books Ltd

Printed in China

www.ladybird.co.uk

DISNEP·PIXAR
MONSTERS, INC.

Ladybird

All children know that night-time is when monsters visit them through their closet doors. What they don't know is that the monsters are just doing their job, collecting children's screams which provide power to their monster world.

The monsters worked for Mr Waternoose, President of Monsters, Incorporated, the largest scream processing factory in the monster world. James P. Sullivan, the number one Scarer at Monsters, Inc. and his assistant, Mike Wazowski, always collected the most screams.

Being a Scarer was a dangerous job. "Never let a kid through one of our doors! Contact with children is deadly!" Mr Waternoose warned new recruits.

Since there was a scream shortage, Mike and Sulley walked through Monstropolis to work.

Mike went to see Roz, the slug-like monster dispatcher At M.I. – who scolded him for forgetting to file his paperwork – before making his way to the Scare Floor. As he and the other assistants ordered up the closet doors, the Scarers entered the Scare Floor.

Randall, who wasn't a very nice monster, wanted to beat Sulley and become the top Scarer.

"May the best monster win!" said Sulley.

"I plan to!" said Randall, spitefully.

The monsters raced in and out of children's rooms, scaring kids and collecting screams.

"Emergency! We have a 2319!" cried the floor manager, as a monster returned with a child's sock on its back. A child's possession was nearly as deadly to monsters as the child itself.

The Scare Floor had to be shut down and decontaminated by the Child Detection Agency, the CDA.

With work over for the day, Mike went to meet his girlfriend, Celia, the company's beautiful receptionist. He was taking her for dinner to celebrate her birthday.

But he'd forgotten to file his paperwork. Sulley offered to do it for him and went back to the Scare Floor. He found a child's door in a Station and whilst trying to investigate, let in a human girl!

After several failed attempts to return the toxic kid, Sulley hid her inside a sports bag. Then he went to find Mike who was on his date with Celia. But suddenly the child escaped, scaring all the monsters in the restaurant!

As agents from the CDA swarmed overhead in helicopters, Sulley and Mike grabbed the girl and escaped to their flat.

Inside, Mike tripped and fell. The little girl giggled, making all the lights flash brightly and then go out. This puzzled Sulley.

Next morning, Sulley decided it would be best to try and put the girl back through her door again.

Dressing her in a monster disguise, he and Mike took her with them to work. The Monsters, Inc. lobby was crawling with CDA agents because they had found Sulley's sports bag at the restaurant.

While Mike tried to find the key to her door, Sulley and the girl played hide-and-seek.

"Boo!" she giggled, running off.

Just as Mike returned to Sulley and Boo (as Sulley had decided to call her), Randall and his assistant arrived.

"Shhh!" whispered Sulley, as they hid just in time.

"When I find whoever let that kid out ..." muttered Randall creepily.

"This is very bad," said Mike, as he and Sulley just managed to get Boo onto the Scare Floor without being seen.

But once again Boo escaped ... and Sulley rushed off to look for her.

As Mike tried to apologise to Celia for ruining her evening, Randall lurked nearby. Overhearing that they had been in the same restaurant as the child, Randall exploded. "Where's the kid? It's here in the factory, isn't it?" he growled.

Under threat, Mike admitted everything.

Offering to make sure that Boo's door would be open, Randall told Mike to return her while the Scare Floor was empty – at lunchtime.

Finding Boo with some little monsters in the company creche, Sulley and Mike headed back to the Scare Floor. But Sulley didn't trust Randall.

Frustrated, Mike opened Boo's door and went through it and into her room to prove everything was safe.

He jumped on the bed, pretending to be Boo. Suddenly, he was trapped inside a box!

Hiding with Boo, Sulley watched as Randall left the room, carrying the box with Mike inside it!

Sulley and Boo followed them into a secret laboratory. Randall strapped Mike to a terrible machine made to extract screams from children.

Sulley secretly unplugged the machine and rescued Mike. Then they ran to find Waternoose.

But as they were trying to tell Mr Waternoose what had happened, he grabbed Boo, opened a door ... and pushed Mike and Sulley through it. Waternoose was in on Randall's plan!

Waternoose had banished them to the human world. Mike and Sulley found themselves on a snowy mountain with the Abominable Snowman, the Yeti!

When the Yeti told them about a nearby village, Sulley had an idea.

He made a sledge out of bits and pieces he found in the Yeti's cave. When Mike refused to go with him, Sulley sped down the mountain alone.

Charging into a child's bedroom and through their closet door, Sulley entered the monster world and raced towards Randall's secret lab, where he found Boo strapped to the machine. Watched by a stunned Randall and Waternoose, Sulley ripped the machine apart and rescued Boo.

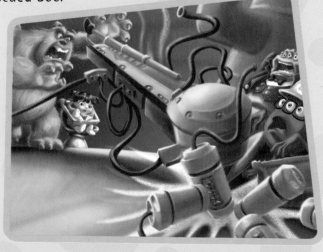

Luckily, Mike had decided to follow his old friend after all, and helped them to escape.

Running to the Scare Floor, Mike explained to Celia what had been happening.

While Celia caused a distraction, Mike and Sulley found Boo's door. But Randall was close behind!

Randall grabbed Boo and then tried to loosen Sulley's grip on the door so he would fall. Suddenly, Boo pulled Randall's head back.

Then Sulley threw Randall through an open door and shredded it so that he could never return!

With a look of pride, Sulley lifted Boo up into the air and laughed, "You did it Boo! You beat him!"

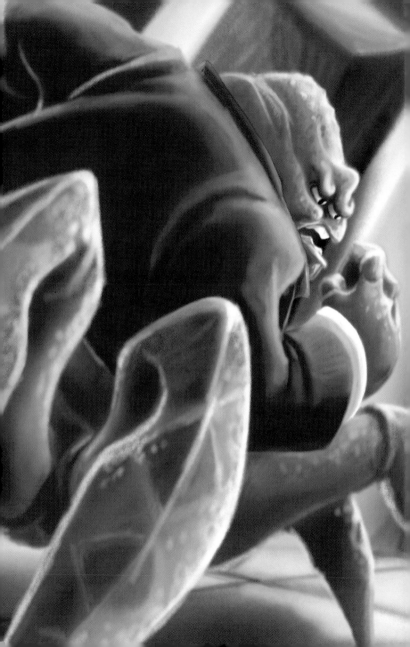

Now it was time to escape from Waternoose. "I'll kidnap a thousand children before I let this company die!" he gasped.

The CDA, who had heard everything, arrested Waternoose, then announced the arrival of their boss . . .

. . . Who turned out to be Roz! She had been working as an undercover agent for the CDA all along!

Roz gave Mike and Sulley five minutes to say goodbye to Boo. Then she would be sent home and her door would be shredded so no monster could ever enter her room again.

Later, when Sulley explained to everyone how Boo's laughter created more power than her screams, Monsters, Inc. was turned into a laughter factory. He was made the president and profits soared.

Sulley still missed Boo. In fact, he was thinking about her when Mike arrived with a surprise for him.

Mike had been busy reconstructing Boo's shredded door! Putting the final piece in place, Sulley walked into the room to find Boo waiting with a big smile. At last they were reunited!